Praise for *Things Happen for a Reason*

"Interesting and informative…A must read!" —Gene Howard, Chief Executive Officer, Orangewood Children's Foundation, The Academy

"It's a truly inspirational story of a former foster youth who persevered after a rough childhood to a very bright future." —Michael Aldaco

"The most honest and real piece of work I have ever read in my entire life." —Elizabeth

"Story of courage and perseverance, a real hero." —Anonymous

"The author takes you a ride through a powerful and affecting story of the challenges foster youth face. Once you pick it up, you won't be able to put it down." —Nick Cunningham, Director and Founder of Generation Fate, Inc.

Things Happen for a Reason

Even Foster Care and Adoption

Kimberly Snodgrass

Edited by Jessica Ernandes

PublishAmerica
Baltimore

Edited by Michael Aldaco.

Hardcover 978-1-4489-8239-4
Softcover 1-60441-544-4
PUBLISHED BY PUBLISHAMERICA, LLLP
www.publishamerica.com
Baltimore

Printed in the United States of America

Dedicated to my family

Acknowledgments

I stand today full of opportunities because people believed in me. I would have never made it this far without a strong team of supporters such as my family, reliable friends, boyfriend, caring professors, scholarships, and academic resources available to me.

Table of Contents

Foreword

When children are in foster care, they sometimes remember what it was like and can have a story to tell. Others permanently erase their memories due to the fact that foster care was not a great memory to remember. This story is about a girl who remembers some good and some bad memories. This story will take you from her first memory as a child to where she stands today, in college.

How I Came to Be

I knew my life was different when I thought raising a child at the age of eight and looking for food in dumpsters to survive was normal, until I woke up. May 12, 1986, Brea, California, out came Amber Ann Reny—that's me. I was born into a world that you would never imagine would happen. Somehow I do not know my father, and I never inherited his last name on the birth certificate. I guess he lives in Michigan, but I have yet to meet him because I feel that at the moment it is unnecessary. As far as the mother goes…I have no idea what got to her, giving me some random guy's last name. I am not supposed to be born Reny! If anything I should at least get my mother's maiden name, which is Pire. Anyway, the whole name thing is a little confusing. I am just an ordinary girl trying to live a very adventurous and fulfilling life.

I need to let you know right from the start, I have a very weird family history so I do not want to get anyone confused. I have a sister Angelina, she is the oldest, I have a brother Nathan, second oldest, me in the middle, a brother Mathew, and a little sister Jessica—she is seven years apart from Mathew. We all have different fathers and two of us are unsure if the ones claimed to be our father are really ours, because my mother cannot remember. I know having so many fathers in and out of our lives makes the mother sound bad, but it's not all 100 percent her fault. My mother was born into an alcoholic family and had a mother who was a prostitute and a father who left her when she was a teenager without giving her the love she needed. Therefore, she found love through other means.

With all that said, I am going to take you on a journey through my life starting with my first memory I can think of. I remember making an Indian costume in Kindergarten with a brown grocery bag. That is the first memory I had while I was enrolled in school. I remember walking around the black top with all of my fellow classmates and dancing around the school as an Indian. Some were pilgrims and some were Indians like me. I only tell you this story because I never got much education in my younger years.

Ever since that memory of school, I keep a vivid picture of my family packing as much as we could in a little tan station wagon and moving away. Why? I had no idea. I was only five. I remember we were in a hurry, packing as much as we could in the backseat, in our laps, and on the floor of the car. I do not know where we went exactly but we went far. We went to the mountains that night.

Now, I know the mountains sound fun, but let me tell you, we were living behind someone's house! I had no idea whose house, I just remember it being in a cabin-like house, all made of wood, but there was no bathroom, and my brother Mathew and I had to sleep in the attic. Now, at this time, I do not remember Nathan or Angelina being in this memory and Jessica was not born yet. I know Angelina and Nathan were taken away from us in the 1980s, but we were not. I know they were in group homes while we lived with the parents at the time of their absence.

So now you have the picture of us living in this cabin and from that I never remember going to school, probably because we were not there long enough to attend. We just packed up in a hurry on Christmas Eve and headed driving down the mountain with all our stuff again. Why? I still didn't know. I did not even think of Santa coming that night, all I wanted was to sleep in a nice warm bed.

At the end of the mountain we stopped at a bar. I do not remember where we were I just know there were lots of dirt roads and at the end of one long dirt road there was a bar. My mom and her boyfriend (Dave) at the time told Mathew and I to stay in the car while they got something really quick. I was tired, so I sat there for a while. It was quiet and dark. Mathew was sleeping on my left leg as I looked out of the window. I decided to push him off gently and go look for my mom and her boyfriend, Dave. I snuck out of the car quietly and opened the big brown wooden door to the bar. There was loud music playing in the background and pool tables to my left. There was also a dart set hanging on the wall as I glanced to my left peeking in the door. No one could see me because I had only cracked the heavy door, and I was little so no one noticed. I saw my mom sitting there with a beer in her hand and slouched over the long table she was sitting at. Dave was shooting darts. I ran over to him and asked if I could play. He told me that I was supposed to stay in the car, but he then told me to just sit there and watch him play for a little bit. I sat there, and continued to be bored. "Can I play already?"

"No! Wait! Go over there with your mother and tell her that you got out of the car," he replied.

"Mom, let's go home already. I want to go home, Mommy," I said in a soft, tired voice.

"Amber! Why did you get out of the car? You are not allowed in here! Go get your butt back in the car and sit there until we leave!" the mother screeched.

"No! Mom, I WANT TO GO HOME!" I screamed with all my might.

"Wait a minute! Go back to the car, Amber! I told you to wait!" screeched the mother again.

I just stood there staring at her as Dave played darts with the wall on the left. By this time I was very angry. I started to pull my mother's leg and scream and whine until she gave up. She was furious with me and grabbed me by the arm and threw me in the car. Click! She locked the car. "Don't come back in here!" she screamed.

I then sat there next to Mathew as he began to wake up from the noise. "Mathew let's go in there and get them. Do you want to go home?"

"Yes, where are we?" Mathew asked.

"I don't know, but I'm scared. Come on, let's go get them," I said softly.

We then went into the bar with no shoes on and stepped over the pebbles in the ground with our bare feet. The night was getting short and cold. There were only a couple of cars in the parking lot. I grabbed Mathew's hand and we hid on the side of the wall next to the door of the bar. We snuck in and then grabbed my mom's leg again and hung on. One on each leg, "Mom, let's go home!" we screamed.

Dave noticed we were making a scene, so he grabbed us, put me in his arms, and Mathew in his right hand. "Let's get out of here. You are so embarrassing!" he yelled at the mother.

We both got yelled at in the car by our mom because we did not listen. We drove out of the bar lot and found a paved road.

We finally reached a motel and stayed there that night. I do not remember having a Christmas, and I do not remember a lot of what happened after that night we packed up again.

15

Next Memories

I know I got bits and pieces of second, third, and fourth grade because we kept moving around, but I never got the full year or even half a year of education. It was always temporary. And when I say temporary, I mean like two or three weeks. Basically my sister Angelina taught me how to read, write, and count. So in this book I am going to take you on a journey (like I said) of all the things I can remember.

Going back into my memory, I have a chunk missing of how Angelina and Nathan got back in our lives since they were missing for a while because they were in the "system." They were taken away that day when we all moved in a hurry from Lake Elsinore, California. Now I know why we were always in a rush leaving places we had lived. It was because my parents at the time were always being evicted! They never paid rent and that is why we ended up living in motels some nights.

Scavengers

Soon after Angelina and Nathan were back in our family, Angelina ran away. Angelina was running away since she was around eight years old. I never did find out where she went or where she ended up. I know some old church friends helped her for over a year and let her and Nathan live in their home whenever they ran away. Angelina never liked staying home, and I noticed she always had problems with my mom because they would always scream at one another. This was not my sister's fault, because when she was the first born child my mother treated her as a drug user. There is a story that Angelina was given cooked medicine (which is a methamphetamine when cooked) as she teethed, so that the mother did not have to hear her whine at night. Angelina was given a life she cold not manage at such a young age, she was doomed from birth to have a messed-up life full of drugs and mishaps. When the mother would be questioned and yelled at as to why she did such things, she laughed it off and claimed Angelina liked it.

We moved again to different mountains over by the Palm Springs, California, area. I remember my parents leaving Nathan, Mathew and me in a blue tent on a hill one day and saying they would be back in a little bit. Well guess what? They never came back. I thought I was there for a day or two, but Nathan told me that they left us for weeks! They left us with no food, but crackers and peanut butter and jelly to eat. I do remember eating those for a very long time. But I had no idea it was weeks because my sense of time was in a different perspective since I was only about five or six at the time they left us. I remember feeling so hungry inside, waiting for something…anything. My brother Nathan always helped us find something to eat. He also kept us warm on the cold nights where we only had our clothes on our backs to keep us warm.

Two weeks later, when the parents came back up to the mountain top they were in a bad mood. My mom was yelling at my little sister's father, Dave, at the time who was with us and she yanked a black cord out of his truck and threw it off the cliff of the mountain. I noticed that they were always in some kind of argument no matter what day of the week it was. They always had something to fight about. She said, "You're not leaving!" and he said, "Watch me!" I had no idea what was happening. Why were they fighting? What happened, and where did they go? I had so many things going on in my young mind at the time. Then all of a sudden my mom took Mathew's shoes and threw them off the cliff as well and said, "They aren't leaving either!"

From that, Dave took me by the hand, and Nathan put Mathew on his shoulders and we started down the mountain to get away from my crazy mother at the time. I do not know where she ended up going, but we walked down that mountain all night long. I remember it being very cold outside and we only had the clothes on our back to keep us warm. Mathew had no shoes so he was being carried down the hill, and I was walking by myself. Occasionally Nathan would put my shoes on Mathew and he would carry me so that I could get a little rest from walking. We walked as far as we could that night until we had no more energy left. I remember my sister's dad saying, "Okay, guys, were gunna pull over now and sleep. We're not gunna make it all the way down the mountain tonight."

So we all stopped and slept in the bushes on the side of the mountain's steep paved road and cuddled together to keep warm. I remember Nathan put me inside his jacket and we fell asleep with Mathew holding on tight as well just trying to keep warm.

Morning came and we started again on our journey down the mountain. We saw only a few cars go by, and then we saw this 4X4 truck coming down the mountain and Jessica's dad stuck out his thumb and we all waved. I was thinking *I hope we get a ride, I really do* because I was tired and exhausted!

The truck luckily stopped and we all hopped in. Then we ended up at Nanny's house. I do not know who she was. All I know is she was Nanny to me. She let us sleep in her other house that she owned on her land in the mountains. We all settled in, and we ate some food.

Somehow later on that night comes my mom rolling in yelling again. "Why the hell did you leave me behind! After all we have been through!"

Why does she always yell I say in my head. She is never happy, they always fight. I didn't like it, it upset me.

Night came along that day and we all went to sleep. This time we had beds to sleep in with warm blankets! I was so happy to have a nice place to stay in. But it didn't last. Nothing ever did.

Morning came and of course we had no food. My mom went down to Nanny's pantry and took some food. I guess you can say she stole it because she didn't ask. What she brought back were beans! Oh man a huge bag of beans! We ended up eating beans and onions for days! For breakfast lunch and dinner!

My mom ended up gathering up more food for us, but it was powdered milk substance, and more beans, crackers and onions! It was getting gross.

Later I found out that we were not only stealing food, but we were not really invited to stay in Nanny's house. I guess we were hiding out.

It was fun being up there for me. I had never thought why I wasn't in school or why I was where I was, but my siblings and I played a lot of games. We went hiking and got stuck with poky things in our feet because it was desert land out there. It never really did hurt when things got stuck in my feet. Sometimes my feet would bleed if I got a big piece of thorn in them, but other than that we were just being adventurous in the mountains.

One day, we went and found water down by a hill, and found some weird stuff in that land that Nanny owned. She had old cars lying around, random things like tools, and a shed filled with other weird tools. We just roamed around looking for things to do; meanwhile our parents were out doing their thing.

If you haven't realized, there is something fishy going on here. I found out later in life that the reason why they were always gone and mysteriously disappearing was because they were on a mission for themselves! To find drugs and alcohol, while we had no food. Very thoughtful I know.

One day while they were gone, we went through their stuff and we found some drugs and some other weird utensils to do their drugs with. I found pieces of glass, burned glass, razors, weird stuff!

So after the whole "Nanny" house we moved again down the mountain to Indio, California. We moved into an apartment where I got lice in my hair for sleeping over at a neighbor's house. I remember being enrolled in third grade, but I didn't stay in third grade very long because we moved again into another apartment in Palm Springs.

After that we just kept moving and moving and moving! It was like a game of life I tell you. I never had many friends because I never stayed long enough to make friends.

Mommy at Eight Years Old

Soon after third grade came to an end for me, Jessica White (my little sister) popped out of my mother's stomach. *Another kid?* I always thought, why would my mother need another child in her life? I mean isn't four enough? She didn't even take care of the four she had! I heard after my mom came home the doctor told her to not have any more children, because if she did she would die. So out comes five, Jessica, and she was just the cutest thing ever! I loved her from the first day my mother brought her home to our house in Artesia.

Well that fun and excitement lasted a good month or so due to my mother dumping her child on me when I was only eight at the time! I didn't even learn how to cook yet, and there I was taking care of little Jessica.

I quickly learned how to change diapers, make baby food, warm bottles of milk, clean up (after everyone), and many more tasks a mother has to learn throughout her life at the age of only eight! I even learned how to taste test the hot food before giving it to the baby.

Now that I look back on those days, I look at Jessica being ten and I just think to myself, "There's no way in hell Jessica could even hold an infant let alone feed one!"

So how did I do it? I do not know, I guess you can say I was forced due to abandonment from both parents at the time. They left us all day most of the time and would come home drunk, fight, and then go to bed. The parents never really had a stable job. They worked for Labor Ready, which is a place where you just show up and work for the day.

By the time Jessica turned one she was able to walk, say a few words, and was on her way to being potty trained. All thanks to me. I was bored staying home all day taking care of Jessica, so I just taught her everything I could with the long days that we spent together.

Fourth grade came around for me, and I do not ever remember being enrolled, so I do not know how long or if I attended school or not. I just remember a few incidents which happened around that time.

One incident that I remember was my sister, who showed up one day out of nowhere! I was so excited to see her. She had a burgundy Mustang car as I remember. I know she had gotten in an accident and got a lot of money and came over to buy me things.

I remember going to her house where she lived with an old guy that she took care of, and I spent the night there for a couple of days. We went to K-Mart and she bought me a big yellow smiley face watch.

After all the shopping we went to a movie where I then lost my favorite watch at the theater! I didn't even own the watch for a whole day until I had lost it. I was so sad about that incident because I never got presents from anyone, so I treasured my gift from Angelina.

Soon after more crying over the watch, I got over it, and we went back to Angelina's place where she pierced my ears. I remember watching cartoons while she said, "Don't worry, the ice will numb it!"

I came back with little simulated diamond earrings. My mom was not very enthused about the idea, but life went on. It wasn't like she ever cared about anything anyway. She always let us roam around on the streets and do whatever we wanted.

Thoughtful Parents...Not

Some nights the parents would stay up all night and play country music really loud. I would ask them to turn it down, and they would bite at me. I could never get peace when I was with them. I was always tired and restless because they didn't care, and I had to do all of the caring. I remember having the chicken pox one night. With the country music blasting in the house, I couldn't sleep. I was wearing a big white tee shirt so the bumps wouldn't hurt so bad. I begged my mom, "Please Mom, please lower the music, it is hurting my ears, I can't sleep!" as I cried.

I was in pain, and they couldn't feel my pain, they were in their own world. I was stuck on earth waiting for my chicken pox to disappear. I had to scratch; it was the only way out of the pain. But just for a moment, then they would come back, and I would have to scratch more. I remember that night trying to sleep but all I could feel was my body aching, and it felt like mush. I didn't feel like I had skin. It was weird. I felt disgustingly sick. I felt like I was dying in my bed, and was lying there to rot because no one would come help me.

The next morning of no sleep I begged my mom for some money or for her to get me some baking soda or something to soothe my pain. She went to the liquor store to get some alcohol and when she came back she handed me a little black bag with baking soda in it. "Here, you happy now?" as she tossed it in the air.

I took it and ran to the bathroom as fast as I could. I dumped the baking soda all over my body mixing it with water. I sat in the bathtub all day. It felt good; the pain was not so bad with the mud mixture that I made. It eventually started to get crusty and thick, so I washed it off and went to bed, which was another unsuccessful night.

Most of the time our place of living was dirty, and I would have the urge to just clean. I would clean all day sometimes because I felt suffocated. I looked around and there would be papers, phone books, trash, food and junk everywhere. I was the only one who felt it was wrong to be in a dirty home.

When the house was dirty some days my mother would jump off the couch and start scrubbing away at everything. I always wondered why she would just get in her "moods." She would clean wall to wall door to door and cabinet to cabinet. She was on a rampage some days. She would pick up everything and organize it, and then reorganize it. I thought she was going crazy when she did these acts because 89% of the time she was a fat, lazy pig on the couch eating away. I would watch her sometimes just eat all day and watch the television.

After thinking she was just in a cleaning mood, I soon realized she was on speed and on fire to clean. She would clean and Dave would flip pages in the yellow phone book all day just looking up names and numbers. I always wondered why, but it was just their thing to do when they got high on occasion. It was mostly when they had the money to get the drugs.

While my mother would be on her cleaning rush, she would make me want to clean so I would help her and clean right next to her. She didn't mind, and I was occupied. Jessica liked to roam around the place with a diaper on and no clothes. Mathew liked to venture out to find things on the street and try to sell them to neighbors to make some cash for food. If we got really bored, we would just dig in the dumpsters of different motels to see what we could find or eat.

One night I spent the night at a neighbor's house in Portola, and I got head lice. I never realized there were bugs in my hair until I took a shower and little black things would fall from the comb and land on the counter and wiggle across. I was disgusted. I took about five showers the night I found out trying the wash them out. They never went away though. I even tried to get a smaller comb to squeeze them out, but nothing worked. I had eventually given the entire family lice. It was sick, but it was bound to happen. We all sleep in the same bed or on the floor most of the time. I never got rid of the head lice, for a long time. I'm talking years of lice.

Strangers

I remember one day when my mom and Jessica's dad (Dave), and their friends came over and they shoved us out of the tiny apartment that we lived in Portola, California, at the time. They sent us out the door with one dollar to get anything we wanted from the 7 eleven up the street. I took Mathew and Jessica in the stroller as we walked up the hill to buy hot cheetos and we put nacho cheese on them. Boy, were they good! I know it sounds gross and all but they were wonderful. We always made new creations with the food we could afford. After all, we were all very tired of eating Top Ramen, beans, and onions!

I remember being in various apartments from time to time in the Artesia, California, area, and remember lots of creepy people entering wherever we lived and stayed there for a couple of days. Some nights I could not sleep because I had insomnia of what the strangers in the house would do to me if I was sleeping. They would always push me around, but I fought back. I did not let anyone tell me what to do. I was a pissed-off little girl. Most of them looked dirty, and I would say all of them smoked right in front of me and blew their smoke in my face. I got used to the smoke after a while. My friends would tell me I stink; I would just reply that I didn't care.

I later realized that the parents just shoved us out so they could shoot up with their friends after shooing us away and off to the store to eat. When we came back one day they had locked us out! I banged on the window and said, "Let us in! What are you guys doing? We're back! Hello! Let us in!"

Jessica's dad answered the door and said, "Wait a few more minutes! Just go! Go somewhere! I have no more money, find something to do."

I was livid inside. "I hate them, I hate them all, I can not believe all of those losers in there. Come along, guys, let's go." I said those words as we walked down the neighborhood with nothing to do but roam round and pick flowers and get wet in the curb where the water drained out onto the streets.

This was not very abnormal for us though. I was used to it, but I was learning slowly but surely what was happening. They had cared less than a penny about their children and loved the drugs they were on more than us. So I knew I had to deal with what I had in life. I just had to suck it up and make the best of it.

Mom and Sister on Drugs

One day Angelina came over at our other apartments that we soon moved into. They were pink buildings with rock walls all around located in Artesia, California. I just remember Angelina going into the bathroom and my mom followed her, and I thought, "What are they both doing in the bathroom?"

With my courageousness that I had built up from putting up with everyone's crap, I barged in! "Why are you guys not coming out?" I yelled.

"Get out, Amber!" my mom yelled as she slammed the bathroom door.

I tried again, but the door was locked this time. I even went and got a butter knife to pry open the door, but it didn't work. I was once again furious at everyone.

After I tried to get to the bottom of what was going on in the bathroom, I gave up. I just sat at the end of the bed and watched TV with Mathew and Jessica. About twenty minutes later Angelina comes out yelling at my mom, and my mom came out yelling back at Angelina. Then suddenly my mom swung at my sister with her hand and my sister dodged her and money flew everywhere.

"What is going on!" I yelled again.

"Shut up!" my mom yelled

"There! Have it! Have it all! I don't care anymore!" Angelina screams toward my mom.

I didn't know how to react. Should I pick up the money that had fallen all over the bed and floor, or should I run away? I jut sat there and looked at my mom picking up the bills off the floor. I was disgusted. I was just curious why my mom and sister were fighting and yelling and then all of the sudden money was everywhere. I soon put all the pieces together and realized that it was the drugs that they were doing! My mom and sister did drugs together! What a great example my mom was to her I always thought (not).

Another memory I have of when I was in this same apartment was when Mathew locked me out. I was over at a neighbor's house and he locked me out when I came back. I saw him inside watching TV, so I knocked on the door as hard as I could to make a loud noise. Mathew started to laugh. He told me to not come back. I did not think this was funny at all so I kept banging on the door yelling for him to open the door. "Mathew, let me in! Let me in! I am going to kill you!" I screamed.

"No!" Mathew laughed.

I persisted on banging on the door which led to banging on the window to the right of the door and continued until Mathew let me in.

Mathew never did open the door. I ended up pushing my hand right through the glass window causing bleeding everywhere and started screaming. Mathew suddenly opened the door and was shocked. He started crying, which made me cry. We were crying because we didn't know what we were going to do. There was glass and blood all over the floor. We didn't know where our parents were or what we should do to get help.

We decided to fix it ourselves. I wrapped my bloody hand in paper towels, locked myself with Mathew in the apartment and called it a night.

I yelled at him about how stupid he was, and then we waited until the parents came home. When they came home, nothing happened to us, they just shrugged their shoulders and asked what happened. We told them, and they just told us to not do that again or we would get into trouble.

Mathew and I looked at each other and then said sorry for being mean and then we went to sleep on the couch in the living room.

That night, they brought over a friend and they slept on the other couch next to Mathew and I. I was so uncomfortable sleeping there, but I had nowhere else to go. I had to hear that person snore and hack up snot in their lungs. It was a man with long dirty greasy hair who was dirty all over and carried a sleeping bag next to him at all times. He was mean and didn't talk much, so Mathew and I ignored him and hid the food from him in another room in the closet the next morning so he couldn't eat. We did not like other people coming in and taking our stuff, especially our food!

Where Did They All Go?

It was the last school day of fifth grade in Artesia, California. I had about a couple months of school there and then school was out and summer was in. I remember walking home and no one was there. There was a sign on the door that said EVICTED written in red ink. Everyone left me, where did my mom go I thought. After seeing that no one was home I went to the owner and said, "Do you know where my family is?"

"No, I don't. I think they went looking for you, but they can't come back here so go find them," replied the grumpy old owner.

So I got my walk on, and headed to school again thinking maybe she would be there to pick me up and maybe I would find my brother Mathew there. When I got there my mother was standing with the stroller in her hands yelling, "Amber! Damn you, Amber! I told you to meet me at the park! Why didn't you listen?"

"I didn't know. What is happening? Where is our stuff?" I cried.

Mathew came jogging over. "Good, I found you! What do we do now, Mom?"

We all didn't know what we were doing. I soon looked over my shoulder and there was a cop walking toward us. "Hi, I was informed that you had lost your mother, and you didn't know where you were going. Are you okay?" asked the cop.

"We're fine, thanks," sneered my mother.

"Well from what I heard, everything is not okay, ma'am, can I have a word with you please?"

"No this is none of your business. Please leave me and my family alone!" yelled my mother.

The cop soon ignored her, put all three of us in the cop car and told us to wait while he figured things out. We sat there for a little while and then told us he was going to take us to a really nice couple, told me and Mathew that we were going to sleep there, and Jessica would sleep with another nice lady. I was confused.

The cop drove us to Desert Hot Springs, California. It ended up that cop car ride put us in the foster care system. I showed up at an Asian family of two, and they were about thirty and could not speak very good English. They were nice though. The next morning after we slept they took us to K-Mart and bought us shoes and clothes for school. I think they had a year-round school so they still had three more weeks left until they got a summer vacation. After buying school stuff they took us to a boxing place and signed us up. I was so excited; I loved the idea so I signed up and bought some wraps for my hands that day.

The first day of me going to the new school with the Asian family was so stupid! No one liked me; I did not make one friend! They all knew that I was the "foster kid." I just ignored them and did my school work to the best of my ability. It was hard, but I kept myself motivated. My brother Mathew said it sucked for him as well, but we tried. Meanwhile I had no contact with Jessica and did not know where she went.

Boxing classes came around the next day after school, and I learned how to punch a punching bag and put on coconut boobs and actually fought a girl my own age. We were just practicing. It was fun for me. Nothing that family did for us lasted though. We soon left after two weeks of living there, and a lady came and took us. She was a social worker.

They Gave Us Back Again

As the social worker dropped us off, I was standing there with a black trash bag in my left hand looking blankly into my mother's eyes wondering *why am I at Motel 6?* This trash bag was not just any trash bag, because it held all of my belongings I had collected over time with different foster families. I held tight to the things that were mine, because my mother left anything we ever owned. I was so mad! I could not believe my mother got us back again! Why were we at a motel? I was so amazed at how stupid the social worker was. Did she really not think it was a bad place, and my mom looked like hell and she was on drugs? Now looking back, I see that it was the '90s and the system was different back then. All a parent had to do was prove that they had a house and food for their children, so we were given back.

Nathan was given back as well from another foster home, and we were all in the motel together. Angelina was still not there. I do not know where she went. I think she was living with church friends that let her live in their house.

That night Nathan packed his black trash bag and whispered, "Amber, I am leaving I can't stand it here, peace out. I am not living with Mom like this. This sucks."

"Nathan, don't leave, please don't leave, it's not that bad. Come on, please stay!"

"Shhh don't wake them up! No, I am leaving. Good night, take care of Mathew and Jessica."

Nathan snuck out of the motel that night and ran away. I did not know where he went, so I just moved on and took care of Mathew and Jessica. As that summer of my fifth grade year passed, we moved to two more motels and we traveled by foot and car. We did motel hopping—that's what I call it. We hopped from motel to motel until the middle of what should have been my sixth grade year in school. I was never enrolled, but I should have been. My mother never cared enough. She left every day and night, and Dave worked every day and went off at night. I never understood them working so much to pay for a motel every night. I know now it was just to have drugs all the time, and a motel was all they could afford and get at the time, since they had bad credit and always got evicted. At least on some nights Dave would come over and give us lunch meat and bread to make sandwiches for dinner and lunch. I made food for Mathew and Jessica and took care of them every day.

We used to go as a family and hop in dumpsters (dumpster diving we called it) in different motels and different dump sites to go trash digging to find cool stuff. We would find all kinds of things! Anywhere from a fake diamond ring to a microwave to a couch!

There would be televisions, books, pens, pencils, sometimes video games, toys, couches and unopened food. We would find all sorts of things from little to huge. We thought it was fun; we did it with our parents too. Sometimes we would dig so fast so that the other person digging would not get our treasure. When we would found something of our interest, we would claim it by saying, "Mine!" and snatch it really fast.

We would also go to food drives and get brown bag lunches and eat those when we could. It might sound weird but I liked the food, it tasted so good to me, but maybe I was just hungry.

Some days my mother would take us to the grocery store, like Albertsons, and tell us to pick any thing we wanted out and to put it in the shopping cart. We would fill the shopping cart sky high and fill it with lots of goodies to eat later on that night. When the shopping cart was all full we would just walk out! We never paid! We stole the food we picked out and walked home! We would all be hanging over the shopping cart walking down the street to our "home." I was used to it, but I now look back and laugh at how crazy that sounds. I do not know how we got away with stealing so much, but we did.

The Night It Happened for Good

It seemed like life was normal by age 11, until one night where it all got a little scary. I was fed up with all of the alcohol and all of the lies and stealing that I took the alcohol and drug pipes and broke them and flushed it all down the drain. My mother came home in the *Red Roof Inn* motel in Westminster, California, and blew up. She went ballistic! She yelled, "Where did my shit go, Dave?"

"I don't know. What shit?" Dave yelled back.

"My stuff and all my drinks. Where is it at? Give it to me! All of it!" she yelled.

Both of them argued for a good half hour. Lisa, my mother, started to hit Dave, so he called the cops and told them what was going on, explaining that she had gone crazy, hurt him and threw things in the motel.

After the phone call, I said, "I did it! I don't know how stupid you think I am, but I did it…no more! There will be no more! I took your pipe, your powder, your alcohol, your everything!"

My mother just stared blankly at me. She did not say anything. She was shocked. Then she blew up again and started yelling at me and Dave and saying that he didn't watch what was going on, everyone was against her, and the whole nine yards.

About another half an hour later, the cops showed up. We were on the second floor. I looked out of the motel window and saw two cop cars and one was knocking on the door.

"Hello, how can I help you tonight?" asked the cop.

"Nothing, everything is fine, bye!" my mother said.

"Ma'am, can I take a look around?"

"No, go away, leave me alone, hey! Don't look at my kids! Go!"

The police officer pushed her aside and looked around in the motel with a big heavy flashlight and snooped around the room. I was just standing there as my mother was yelling in the back of the room, and then another cop came up the stairs and tried to arrest her. She fought back and pushed the cop.

"Don't touch me! Get your hands off me! Bastard!" she yelled.

He locked her hands up behind her back and put the cuffs on her. She could not resist. I saw that he was a lot stronger than her.

After she was handcuffed she was taken into another room and was talked to by a cop to figure out what was going on. She told him nothing so the cop came to ask me what was going on. He explained why he was there at the motel and looked down upon me sitting on the bed.

"Are you happy?"

"No…" I said while I was thinking in the back of my head, *should I even tell him that I am unhappy because he might take me away again and I don't want that.* I was nervous, but I told him the truth. We talked about everything, and I told him what I did and he was happy that I knew it was wrong.

"Do you want to leave?" he asked softy.

I said, "Well…yeah, I kind of do…" so then he grabbed me by the hand.

"Come with me, you guys are going be okay, don't worry."

He then told my brother Mathew and my sister Jessica to hop in the cop car. The young policeman said, "Don't worry kids; you will see your parents tomorrow."

Taken Away

I thought nothing of what he said, so I just sat in the cop car while we went through the drive through of KFC to get some dinner for us. After about thirty minutes we arrived at the police station where my mother had met up to as well, and they took down our names and placed my mother in another room. We were then driven to a place called Woodorange Children's Foundation. I had never heard of this place before, but they made us turn in all of our belongings on us, and made us wear their clothes while they marked on a paper what marks we had on our body like bruises and such.

As we stayed in Woodorange, in Riverside, California, we were treated like prisoners. We ate the same food, wore the same clothes and had to do everything on a timely manner to get our good start for the day. Some children were banging there heads on the walls. I just ignored it. We were all separated into different age categories and by sex. I was in a girls home, Mathew was in a boys home, and Jessica was in a baby home—she was almost two. I had received my very first bra there. It was weird. They told me I needed a bra and asked why I didn't wear one, and I told them that I never wore one and I was fine. They didn't think so, which is why I was made to wear one to hide my little boobies which we growing. I had to get good behavior stars so that I could volunteer in the nursery to visit Jessica. Sometimes I would go to do dishes, and I would just watch her nap and I would never see Mathew because they didn't let me. We visited my mother at Woodorange two times, and then one month passed and my siblings and I got picked up by the Sanders family. Someone just said one day, "Hey, someone is here to take you, they will be your new family." I remember that day of them getting us, they didn't have Mathew, and they didn't even mention him. When Ann Sanders overheard the conversation that Jessica and I had a brother she told the social worker that she would take him into the home as well. They were all surprised that she had talked three kids to be in one foster home. We were always separated because no one wanted that many kids. So Mathew was brought into the room where we had all met the new foster parents, and we left to their home in a blue minivan.

All I could think was oh, great another family, whatever. I sat in the car quiet the whole car ride until we reached La Hibra, California. When I got there to their home, there were dogs, cats, and birds everywhere! It looked like a zoo. The backyard had like 100 birds in aviaries. I didn't like it, it smelled like animals, and I felt uncomfortable once again. I was in a place where I was forced to be, and unhappy. Ann Sanders told us to call her mom. I told her no! I was mad that she wanted me to call her that, she was not my mom! Eventually I started calling her mom and so did Mathew and Jessica. We slowly eased into calling her mom and Branden Sanders dad.

It was the weekend and we all went school clothes shopping and tried to remove the head lice from back when I was eight. The lice were infested in my head and were very hard to get out. We tried a couple of the chemicals with different boxes to kill the little bugs. Woodorange had tried to remove the lice, but they just came back. After Ann removed all of our sheets, blankets, pillows, clothes, and other belonging and put them in the trash the lice seemed to settle down and disappear. She bleached all of our combs, threw away all of our brushes and other things in the house. She also bleached the entire home to sterilize all of the furniture to get rid of it. It was bad, so after shaving Mathew's head, cutting mine and Jessica's hair and sterilizing the house, we finally got rid of the nasty little bugs.

Ann Sanders bought us all new clothes and shoes and stuff for school. I liked all of the shopping, but it wasn't anything I didn't already know. My sister and I slept in a room together and Mathew was never told to Ann until last minute so she had to have him sleep on a cot for two days until the other little kids moved out. After that weekend of being in the Sanders' house I was enrolled that Monday in 1996 to sixth grade. It was December 11, I remember. I hated it. Once again I was at a school where no one liked me because I came in the middle of the year and had no friends. I remember playing basketball and I stepped on this little girl's foot who was in my class at the time, and she cried. No one liked me after that day, they called me a bully. I was just an aggressive person who wanted to be the best at everything and I was a little big in sixth grade. They didn't like me. I only had one friend who was a nerd just like me, and we talked about God a lot and hung out every day together. My grades were not so good in sixth grade. I was behind. I was getting C's and a little A's and B's. I was upset because I tried really hard. By the end of that sixth grade I had caught up for the most part, and my teacher was happy to see me grow. My neighbors did not like me and neither did kids at school.

Junior high came around and I was still in the Sanders home. By this time, my foster mom received two young children, Becca and Allan. They were a sibling set. They came into the system at age 10 and 11, just like me and Mathew when we first moved into the Sanders home. Allan was older; Becca was younger by one year. They came in from their mother doing drugs and alcohol as well. I loved them at first because we were all around the same age and we got along well with one another. Becca came in overweight and so did Allan, but not as much as Becca. I remember the first night they ate with our Sanders family. We had homemade spaghetti and French bread. I remember looking across the table seeing the two siblings, Allan and Becca, heaping their food into their mouths as if it was the last time they were going to eat. They had first helpings, then second helpings, then third helpings of mountains of spaghetti! I was astonished, and so was our foster mom. She told them to eat as much as they wanted, but she also advised them to slow down before they choked. We all giggled as we viewed them hording it all in. I realized though, they were still thinking like most foster kids do; it could have been their last meal. You never know what you are going to get when you move around a lot. Their former foster parents were mean and made them eat left over food all the time and canned soup. They also said they did not get new clothes like they were supposed to. Some foster parents can be on your side or can be on their side. Only out to help themselves. Some foster parents take the money they get from the kids they take care of and use it for their own benefit, and not the child's! I hated hearing some of those stories about bad foster parents! It just made me sick! How stupid the foster system could be to treat children that are not even theirs! Some only cared about the money. It was sad. Allan and Becca ended up living with us for a long time after that. We all grew up together sharing memories of stealing food and games to play with from food stores. Allan and Becca told me about their first kiss and how they got to roam around the streets just like us. We almost compared our life stories together and laughed at how cool we were and how no one watched us.

During this same time, my birth mother was still not getting her act together and was too into herself and her drugs. Social workers and other services tried to give her affordable housing and parenting classes to help her get better, but it took her a long time to accept them.

Seventh grade came and went and I made some friends. I met my best friends Jessica, another girl Jessica, and Alicia. I joined band because I had always wanted to, and I borrowed a flute from the band teacher and took it home to the Sanders' house. I was so excited I learned the flute in one day I loved it and instantly knew how to play it. I do not know how, but I was magically talented with it.

I continued the flute into eighth grade and became first chair (which is the best) and began to have a passion for music. From then on, I was earning almost all A's by the end of eight grade and some B's here and there.

Stuck

Time passed. I ended my eight grade year, and was entering high school. I remember my social worker coming to the house and wanted to talk to me because I was the oldest with my foster mom, Ann, at the time. We walked down the hallway and into Ann's room. I sat on the end of the bed, Ann sat in a chair next to me, and the social worker was standing talking to both of us. She had papers in her hand and not a smile on her face. She was just plain looking. I knew something was not right, but I didn't know what was wrong. "Amber, the reason why we took you in here alone, is because you can understand what is going on, and I think you should know before this prolongs," the social worker said looking at me.

"Okay, go head…what is it?"

"Well, this is not good news, but I legally have to tell you. You see, your mother, Lisa, was given one last drug test to complete the process to get you back… And she did not pass her test. I am sorry, Amber. You and your brother and sister will now go into a process which will prolong your stay here with the Sanders family," she said.

I sat on the bed with an empty heart. I sank to the edge as the blankets fell down with me. Ann looked at me and said, "Come here, baby, it's okay, don't cry, things will get better."

She then gave me a big bear hug, and we held each other for a while. Tears ran down my face in streams. I was devastated. I buried my head into Ann's chest and sobbed in sorrow. I couldn't believe my mother was so stupid to do drugs right before her test, and right before we were so close to go home with her.

After crying, I looked up to the social worker and said, "What happens now?"

"Well, your mother has to appear in court, and then the judge will make his decision as to her parental rights. Your mother may get another chance to get you back, or she may loose all her parental rights to you and your siblings. If that happens…you guys will be put up for adoption."

I just swallowed what the social worker said to me and took a big gulp. I didn't want to face the fact that my mother had just ruined the only chance for us to get out of the foster care system. I just put my head down and walked out of the room.

"I will be fine, just leave me alone for a little while," I said as I dragged my feet across the wooden floor.

Ann and the social worker told my brother and sister after I left the room. They were not happy. Jessica didn't really even know what was going on, and Mathew was just acting like nothing happened. He seemed confused and just stayed quiet that day. He had a tendency to just hold it all in.

We transitioned into monitored visitation, and my birth mother missed a lot of those visits because she didn't have a ride, or she forgot. She would come to a lake by the Sanders' house and visit for about two hours. We had to bring along Ann Sanders to monitor us. We would play games like golf and Frisbee. The visits were always just a re-cap of what we were doing in school and the same old questions over again. They always said they were proud of us…but they never did any thing to show it. I always thought if they were really happy for us and appreciated the hard work we did in school, that they would get their act together and get us out of the system.

High School

Freshman

My freshman year in high school was fun. I joined the marching band and concert band and made even more friends. The summer going into high school I had to practice music in band camp. I started to be around a different environment, such as guys, drugs, nice people, mean people, weird people, and popular people. During this time I was faced to choose a path for myself. I tried the whole guy thing…but it didn't work for me. I thought this one boy was so cute and I found out he liked me back, so we tried to be boyfriend and girlfriend. It didn't work out though. The "relationship" lasted for like a day! I broke up with the guy because I was not ready to give for any emotions. I did not like hugs, or holding hands, or kissing! I remember everyone in high school making fun of me because I was such a prude! I didn't care though. I did not feel comfortable, so I kept my ground as to who I was. I was Amber, and that was it. If I didn't want to be an emotional person, then I didn't want to be just like everyone else. It took me a long time to give my friends hugs and my foster parents hugs or kisses.

During my freshman year, I also enrolled in roller hockey because that is just what the Sanders did: they all played hockey. I remember watching the Sanders' children John and Nathan at their hockey games, and I thought it looked like fun! Branden Sanders encouraged me to join, and then we got Mathew and Jessica to join as well. We all loved it, and it kept us active. As my first quarter as a freshman I received really good grades. I got all A's and one B+. I was really excited, which made me try even harder to get straight A's. I stayed in band and still had a desire to love music, which led me to think that I wanted to be a music major and teach music as my career. Around this time, Rebecca and Allan were given back to their birth mother. They only stayed for about a month, and were sent to Woodorange again. Ann Sanders found out, and picked them back up and then took them into their house again to stay as foster children. Their mother got back on drugs, and that is where their journey in foster care got even longer, just like the rest of us in the house.

During the middle of my freshman year, I learned how to play the saxophone, the obo from my mom, a little clarinet from my dad and I enrolled in jazz band. I was loving all of the music and started to get really involved in school and finally earned my straight A's which I had been wanting all my life. By this time I was about 14 going on 15 and my mother was just going downhill losing all her rights and missing more visits each time we scheduled to meet. I joined a Marketing and Business Academy in high school and became a member of a business association, while continuing to play in band and play hockey.

Towards the end of my freshman year, I was finally reunited with my long-lost brother Nathan and sister Angelina, they are both around eight years older than me. They brought me, Mathew, and Jessica presents and we all had lots of fun. We were all excited to finally see each other. It had been so long. We instantly brought back our childhood and remembered that we were brother and sister once again. The day was filled with laughter and tears as we reminisced about the past.

I Wanted Everything

Sophomore

One day Ann bought me some jeans. They were spread across my bed when I came home. I liked the surprise, but when I saw that they were a size nine I freaked out! I couldn't believe she thought I was so fat! I remember trying them on and showing her how baggy they were on my legs. I stood in Ann's room and said, "Mom, look I do not fit in these!"

"Honey! You're not a size five any more! Get over it. They look fine on you. They are not supposed to be painted on your skin ya know!" she said with a magazine in her hands and she sat in her recliner looking at me through her eye glasses.

I ran to my room and cried. The room was dark and I just laid on my bed and put my head into my pillow. *I hate her! I hate me too. I don't want to be fat!* I thought to myself.

Ann walked into my room about five minutes later and said, "Are you really hurt over this, Amber? I didn't mean it like that. Honey, you are turning into a woman! Guys go into goo goo land when they look at you! You have an hourglass figure, and that is what is supposed to happen at your age. You are not fat in any way. Please forgive me, I didn't mean to make you feel this way."

I decided to get skinny and Ann Sanders was scared because she thought I went anorexic. I didn't think so at the time, but she was scared so she watched over me. One day she made me eat in front of her. It got so bad she started to weigh me every week. She told me if I lost at least one pound, she was going to put me into a hospital! I was just becoming too much of a perfectionist that year. I wanted everyone to accept me, and I wanted to be the best I could be. I started to eat apples for breakfast and lunch and Cheerios for snack. I was way determined to prove her wrong and to wear a size five again or even smaller. I counted every calorie and read every package of food to make sure

I didn't eat too much in one day. I almost became obsessed. I got over the whole eating disorder thing, or I hid it for a while going into the next years in high school.

As my sophomore year came around, I went through some crazy times of my life. I was put up for adoption because my birth mother had lost all of her legal rights to all of her children. Ann and Branden Sanders did not want to adopt because they were getting old and they were unsure if they could handle all of us.

I remember Ann having a talk with me and saying that she almost adopted two little boys, but she didn't because she felt that she was too old. After we found out that we were up for adoption, Branden and Ann sat us down in the living room to tell us what they thought about our time in the system.

"The social worker gave us two options. One, you can live with us (the Sanders), and we will take guardian care of you until you all turn eighteen. Or two, you all can be adopted by us. Branden and I have thought long and hard about the process of adoption and the process of guardianship...and we feel that it is in everyone's best interest to...well...we would like to adopt you. All three of you! What do you think about that?"

I was kind of freaked out, but at the same time I felt a sense of relief. I knew instantly that I was going to be okay. I looked at my brother and sister and smiled. We all didn't know what to do. We just sat there on the couch and looked around.

"That sounds good," I said as I smiled and stood up from the couch.

Ann then stood up and said, "Come here, guys." She then gave all of us a huge hug and Branden then joined us too.

He smiled and said, "Hey...! You want to be a Sanders?"

We all giggled with little tears running down our faces. Jessica still didn't realize what was going on. She just went with the flow and hugged the new parents too.

At this time, Allan and Rebecca were still living in our home and they were confused because we were all being adopted, and they were still foster children. They figured out what was going on and accepted all of us.

The Adoption

By my sixteenth birthday, and my sophomore year of high school, I was adopted along with Jessica and Mathew by the Sanders (hence my last name now). I remember being pushed around by the lawyer as he asked me if I was brainwashed by the Sanders to be adopted. He kept asking me over and over again if I was sure that I wanted to be adopted. I continued with yes to the repetitive questions. The man made me cry, and I was confused with his tricky questions. He was filling my head with weird thoughts. I remember walking out of the courtroom feeling sick to my stomach. I was tense with knots in my back. I did not want to go back into the courthouse, but I had to. We waited for Mathew to testify and the lawyer came out in the lobby to grab Jessica and said that the mother would like to have Jessica testify. My adopted mother looked firmly into the lawyer's eyes.

"No! She is only five. There will be no way my little girl is going to be badgered while looking at her mother in court; she doesn't even know what is going on!" she said.

The lawyer just looked down and insisted. As he was pushed away the second time, he gave up. The last time I had to go into the courthouse was to sign the official papers. I remember feeling really happy during the signing and my mom and dad who adopted me were glowing with joy. My father, Branden, did not really show it, but I could feel it. At the end of the signing the judge gave all of us a stuffed animal. The lawyer threw mine at me and said, "Here!"

I just took the teddy bear and smiled. "Thank you…"

After the adoption, we had a huge celebration at our house. The neighbors, church friends, our school friends, and family came over to congratulate our new family. It was fun and exciting; we ate cake and opened many cards that people gave to us with warm wishes into our new family. I was so happy that day. I remember thinking to myself that now I have a family that will stay together. No more moving around, no more wondering where I will be. And the best part, no more wondering if I will get to eat or sleep somewhere. The comfort was set in, I knew I was in a loving family.

No More Two Mothers

My mom (now Ann) promised to keep in contact with our biological family, but soon after getting adopted, I lost contact with my birth mother, and set out to make something of myself. I remember waiting for my birth mother for a visitation with our social worker one day. We drove to *Jack N the Box* to meet her there. We waited for an hour, it was pouring rain. As we stared into the window with a big hamburger on the other side, all I saw was nothing. It was getting dark and the rain was getting worse outside. I was bored sipping my creamy milk shake that my social worker bought me. *When is she coming? Don't tell me she is just going to leave us in the rain with her nowhere to be found!* I thought. My social worker told us that we will all wait 5 more minutes, and if our mother didn't come she would take us back home to the Sanders. Those five minutes flew by, the mother never came, and I just held my frustration inside and stepped into the car. I was staring blankly into the car window trying to picture my mom running to me yelling, "Wait, wait, I'm here!" But she never came. I must have been delusional to think of that. I knew how she was. I knew she had left Nathan and Angelina. What made the three of us any more special than them? Why would she visit three kids, if she never visited the others? She had a long reputation of abandonment. I should have known not to think she would come. I got over it and just prepared for the worst. I prepared that I would never see any of my birth family again because they didn't care about us. My mother now, Ann, told me she remembers me coming home on our last visit with the parents that we ever had. She said I looked like I got beaten up because my eyes were purple and red. I was a wreck with tears so wet, my hair was stuck to my face. She told me she remembers me being so upset that she got upset watching me, and we cried in each other's arms that day. I don't know why I was so upset; I tried to fade that memory as well. I know I was angry because I was accepting the fact that I would never have what I used to think was family. Eventually the Sanders family just became my only family. I had forgotten about the others since they never came to visit me. I had accepted the fact that my own mother did not want her children, not even to visit them.

Sophomore

During the end of my sophomore year in high school, I found a job, KDW Uniforms, which was right next to my high school and I worked there for my very first job. I loved it, and they loved me. We ended up making a little family in that job that I had. They treated me with respect and loved the fact that I was a hard worker. I had saved all of my paychecks for the entire summer going into my junior year, I bought a car, a license, and paid for my car insurance all by myself. After getting the job, as working at a uniform store, I decided to get even busier and stay in hockey and join the church band to keep me really busy so that I would never get into trouble. I also became the president of our student store while being in the business program in high school.

Later on that same year, Allan and Becca were adopted too due to their mother losing her parental rights as well. In acceptance to the adoption, we had the opportunity to be in every year of high school with one another. I was going to be the senior; Mathew was the junior, Allan the sophomore, and Becca the freshman. We were excited to get to grow together and be in high school with each other. There had been no siblings like this before in our high school. We were able to have four Sanders in one school now with their adoption! After all of the paperwork and the whole process of adoption, we all laughed at how many brothers and sisters we had just accumulated. We now had the Sanders siblings, which were Julie, Tiffany, John, and Nathan, then we had Angelina, Nathan, Amber, Mathew, and Jessica from our adoption that June, and then we created even more by the adoption of Allan and Becca who had Alison and Stacy (their sisters). We had accumulated 13 brothers and sisters! It was fun to tell everyone at first, and then we got over the excitement that our mother had just adopted five kids! At this time, may I mention, we also had four dogs and four cats! The house was really crowded, loud, and there was lots of hair and dust from the animals. I grew a dislike for animals since we had too many, and any time I got dressed I had to worry about dog and cat hair everywhere.

Junior

I joined National Honors Society and more clubs on campus to get ready for college. I knew I wanted to go, but I didn't know where or what to do to get there. I just knew deep down I would get there and I would go. I ended up becoming more active in my high school and was accepted to become the president of the student store with the business academy at the high school I was attending. I kept my grades up, and continued music and hockey. I kept in touch with all of my friends that I had since junior high. Alicia and Jessica were big supporters of me as I continued throughout high school. They always kept my head up when it was down. We would all share memories and they accepted some of my horrific memories and did not look at me any different than the rest of our friends.

The Boyfriend That Would Last Forever

At the end of my junior year I had met a guy named Mitchel, who then became my boyfriend. This is how he thinks we have a love story, he wrote this to me:

Okay so I was at the Chinese fast food store one day, and I was ordering food for my family when I saw this girl named Amber in there. She was president of her high school business program. She was buying Chinese food for a reception for her school company when I said to her, "So I see you're hungry, huh?"

"Yeah, you too?" Amber said as she saw me holding two big bags of food for my family.

That was it! We never saw each other again.

Roughly two weeks later, I got a phone call from my good girl friend Jessica to ask for directions using her friend Amber's cell phone. I had forgotten about the phone call and called that number one night to see who it was who called me on my cell phone one day. When I called, it was a girl. I said "Hello? Who is this?"

Then she replied, "You called me, who is this?"

I said, "Well your number was in my incoming calls...and I didn't have a name for the number in my cell phone, so who is this?"

She then said, "Amber, but I don't think I know you...who are you...what is your name?"

I then replied, "I can't tell you...where do you live? What city?"

"La Hibra," Amber said.

"Me too...where in La Hibra?" I said.

"Why?" Amber said.

"Just curious if I might know where you live," I said (Mitchel).

"I live on Wilshire Ave," Amber replied.

"You mean the street with the dead end and a basketball hoop at the end of your street?" Mitchel said in surprise.

"Yes! How do you know that?" Amber exclaimed.

"I live on Baja!" yelled Mitchel.

"So we are neighbors?" Amber said.

"I guess so…" Mitchel said.

"Hey…do you want to meet each other since we are neighbors after all? Just so I can get a look at who I am talking to, I mean you are my neighbor and all…what could be the harm?" Amber said cautiously.

The next day Amber and Mitchel met after school at around 4:00 on a Friday, May 7, 2004. They immediately noticed that they had seen each other somewhere but couldn't put it all together.

"The Chinese food store!" Amber yelled.

"That's it!" Mitchel said.

So they went on their date to speed zone after meeting each other and hit it off well. They thought they would never see each other again and here they were…on a date.

So that is how Mitchel says we met, and I agree. After meeting this new guy, the same year of me being sixteen—turning into seventeen (my birthday came fast), things were becoming more serious, and I told him about my crazy life. He was supportive and encouraged me during everything.

During our adventurous dating days when Mitchel and I would go out and have fun like every other teen who we hung out with, something happened. This is another incident that I will never forget.

It was around 11:30p.m. I should have been home, but I was with Alice, my best friend, and I was going to spend the night at her house, until I got this phone call. I was so excited I yelled to Alice, "It's Mitchel, should I answer?"

"Yes! Pick up your phone!" Alice screamed back at me.

I answered the phone, Mitchel told me he was at a party, and he wanted to know if I would go over and pick him up. I said yes without hesitating and drove over there. I got to the party around midnight and it was over, Mitchel hopped in my car and we were off to go back home. Well we didn't get there as fast as we thought.

There were these girls on one side of the street with a couple of guys and they were screaming and jumping around having fun. Mitchel was a little hyped up at the time so he was laughing in my car looking at the people outside. I drove away with my stick shift car. I was going pretty fast by now and we were away from the people, which is what I wanted.

All of the sudden Mitchel grabs my steering wheel and yanks it to the right. I got scared and pulled it back to the left. We were going so fast that the car locked up and I overcorrected his pull and we went swerving. It was like a slow motion curve in my memory. I hit the brakes but nothing happened, it was if they didn't work! I saw ahead cars, homes, and trees. I was scared, I just held on to the steering wheel screaming, "Oh my gosh!" As the car pushed through my control we crashed into a huge tree next to someone's house. The impact was so hard that the car was smashed up to my steering wheel. I saw the tree coming, and I could not control the car. I saw it coming from so far away, but I could not stop. After we hit, I looked at Mitchel and just screamed. "My parents are going to kill me! This is a dream right? Right? What did you do?! Oh my gosh! What am I going to do! My car is ruined!"

Mitchel just looked stunned at me as I went into panic mode. I didn't know what to do. We sat there looking at each other as we were crushed in the car. We took off our seat belts and tried to get out. I was not that stuck, so I wiggled out, and Mitchel found a way out as well. The adrenaline was running so high I was just freaking out as I looked at my car drip oil and smoke against the tree. I just cried and stared. I could not stop thinking about what I was going to do and what I was going to tell my parents.

A lady came out of the house we crashed by and offered us help. She called the police and gave us a drink. She was a nice lady and tried to calm us down. I was still in shock though. About 20 minutes later, four or five police cars arrived. They had their sirens and lights bright on us. I was so embarrassed and scared. As one police officer came up to me, the first thing he said was, "You know...this is city property, you are going to have to pay for this tree ya know?"

I was like, "What? Why would you tell me that! We just got into an accident and that is what you are going to tell me?" I was freaking out. I could not stop crying, so Mitchel had to tell the officer what had happened.

The report came to be that Mitchel saw an animal in the street so he pulled my wheel, and I over corrected it. I never saw an animal, but Mitchel says he did, so I went with it. That was our story of how we wrecked my car.

After the report, I called my dad and told him to come pick me up, and that I was in a mess. I told him I would explain later, but he needed to come right away. At this time my parents did not know who Mitchel was, they didn't even know where I was at the time. I had to introduce Mitchel to my father in front of our tree accident. It was as humiliating for him as it was for me. We called our insurance company and they picked up my car. After that, my dad gave Mitchel and me a ride home, and I got yelled at–no screamed at. When I came home, my mom was still asleep and my dad just told me to go to bed.

When morning came, the entire house had known what had happened and they were all screaming at me. My mom went ballistic on me. She screamed and yelled and asked what I was doing with a boy in the middle of the night, and who he was, and got all of the details out of me. I was crying and told her I was sorry, I didn't mean for this. She kept yelling, and sat me outside with my dad. We discussed why I did it, and how it happened, they didn't really believe me, but it was the truth. They decided to give me a month's restriction in the house. I could not leave for a month. I was sad, upset, and so confused of this slow-motion accident that I will never forget.

That day, I walked myself to work, and cried the entire way there. All I could think about was that I had no car. I worked and saved every penny to buy my first car, and what did I do...ruin it all. I hated that day, I hated work, and I hated my life. I really felt like I didn't want to live. I was not suicidal, but I felt so bad that I did not want to keep thinking about it.

Later that same day, Mitchel came over, met my mother and sat with her and my dad. They discussed what happened, he apologized and said he would pay my deductible from the accident. They agreed and liked the fact that he had enough courage to come over and apologize. We later found out that my car was totaled and I had to get a new one. I got money back from my accident, saved the money that I had earned, and went to get another car.

Mitchel, my dad, and I went to the auction and picked out another car. This was a month later; remember I was on house restriction? I hated that month. But, we got over it, and the memory slowly faded from my parents' memories, and they finally let me have my life back. They ended up accepting Mitchel as my boyfriend and welcomed him into our house. It took Mitchel a long time to feel comfortable in my house, but we pulled through and accepted it.

What About Angelina?

My sister stopped visiting, and we wondered if she had gotten back into drugs with my mother. I eventually found out with a knock on the front door as to why she had stopped visiting us.

It was my brother Nathan and his fiancée Aly. "Hey guys, listen we need to talk," he said sluggishly. He had looked like he had been hit with a bat and run over by a truck. His eyes were red and his face was drowsy. My heart was pounding. I instantly started feeling cramps in my stomach from stress and my blood was pumping inside. I wanted to know what the hell happened to my brother. He took a seat on the left of me holding a bible and some papers. I stared into his eyes as he started to cry.

"Angelina is dead, guys. She…she died!" sobbing now in tears Nathan cried out.

I instantly blew up. Bursting in tears, No! No! No! This is not happening, where is she? No! No! No! How? Why? No! I was screaming by now in tears. I was so hurt inside. This was worse than losing my birth mom. Angelina was my mom; I loved her with everything I had. She had taught me everything I had ever known. Why did this just happen to me I asked. Jessica looked at me and started to cry. She did not know why she was crying, but she cried because I was crying. Mathew was on my right sitting on another couch and sobbed quietly.

I ran out of the room, and cried into my pillow sitting on my bed. I soaked it with tears as I felt the worst pain I had ever experienced in my heart. I was devastated. I could no longer go on I thought to myself.

I came back into the living room where they were sitting with Nathan. Nathan then explained that she was on drugs with my mother that night at a party. Angelina wanted to leave, but the mother wanted to stay. Angelina left without her. Then she had called my birth mother that night telling her that she could not stay awake, but she insisted on driving home to her husband. She didn't make it home that night. She drove off the road into a tree while driving on the freeway in Palm Springs and pronounced dead at the scene.

My brother Nathan gave me the bible and said it was Angelina's and it was her first. He also had a picture of her in his other hand and said, "This is all I have of her." He had a news article inside the picture and told me that it was dated two years ago. I didn't get it. Why didn't we get a phone call or anything to know about her death? All this time I had thought, she was just too busy for us. I was wrong, she was dead. All I could do was weep about it and think of nothing else. Nathan explained that no one had a funeral for her because there was no money, so they cremated her and her husband got to keep her ashes. I could not believe that no one did anything for her, not even notify her own family about her death! I was so confused and upset that we had to find out this way that my sister would no longer come to visit me and give me hugs and kisses. I just wished I could have said good bye to her and told her that I loved her one more time before she died. I could not accept the fact that she was gone permanently. That night I cried myself to sleep; I prayed to God and told him I was broken.

Senior Year

I slowly got over the death of my sister and learned to cope with death…(well sort of). My senior year came around, 2005. I was getting ready for everything. I was saving for my car insurance and money to move out and get a laptop for college and to start my new life as an adult. I continued hockey, band, the church band, and I made it to becoming the CEO of the Marketing and Business Academy (MBA) program of our high school. I was the CEO of a virtual business and loved doing what I did my senior year. I was also published in two books for my grades and what I was doing in high school. I was published in *Who's Who of America,* and *National Honors Society.* My family was happy for me, as I was for myself. I didn't know how to apply for college, but I found out on my own. The internet was my best friend. I learned everything on it. I called lots of people from Woodorange and found out that I could get money for being a former foster child. I then called more people and applied to the University of California, Los Angeles (UCLA). The day I applied on the internet, it cost $50.00 so I said to myself, *What? That's a lot of money! I guess I will only apply to one since that is all I have.* I knew my mom didn't have money to give me because I had to pay for my own SAT test! Which by the way I did horrible on! I scored lower than anyone I think. I don't remember what the score was, but it was around 1,000. I hated tests, and I didn't take the SAT very seriously. I was not in the mood to take the stupid test anyway because I had almost gotten into a car accident driving to the test site. I had to drive to Compton, California, because I signed up late, and there were no close places to take the test. I was confused and accidentally got on the wrong side of the road trying to get there. I almost died! But I swerved and made it out of the car's way.

I didn't know that it was actually hard to get accepted into a university until the end of the year came around and everyone was nervous to get in. I then got a little worried because I had only applied to one university. The month of May came around that year, I turned 18, and I graduated high school with honors and got accepted into UCLA. I was so excited I think I tinkled in my pants with pee a little bit when I found out. I was so excited being that I was the only one in both of my families getting to go to a university. I knew I had always wanted to go to college, and so I did. I then received a full ride including housing and tuition.

At my graduation party, my parents surprised me and bought me a laptop! I had no idea they were going to get me one, so that gave me a chance to save some money for other stuff like dorm items such as sheets, pillows, clothes, books, and supplies. I was set for college. I ended the year still working at the same uniform store and still with the same boyfriend, Mitchel, who started college that same year, but not the same one as me, he went to a junior college.

Before I entered college, after I graduated my older brother Nathan got married to his wife, Aly, that June of 2005. She is a science teacher with a master's and working on her doctorate to become a doctor. Nathan works in construction and is planning to open his own pet grooming store. Nathan has a driven heart to not let anything get in his way. He had a rough childhood, some stories in which I have never heard of since he has so many, but he does not let any of them keep him down.

Freshman Year in College

Before actually starting college, I was given an opportunity to meet with one member of the university all to myself. His name was Jim; I will never forget his name. He told me over the phone that he wanted to meet me to see if my head was screwed on straight. I laughed and met him a few weeks later. He gave me another insight to what college was all about. He asked me if I wanted to leave the country, I replied with a NO! But I eventually started taking some of his advice, because it was all for my own benefit.

Everything was finally piecing together for me, I was enrolled in full-time summer school for UCLA that same month I graduated, June of 2005 for an intensive summer bridge program to get me prepared for UCLA. That program was so strict too. They did not let me talk on my cell phone or have my car. They kept us there doing lots of work and a bus schedule. I don't think it helped me, but it was hard. I made a couple friends in that program, but one girl I really seemed to like. Her name was Fanny. She seemed like a cool chick, so I roomed with her that first year going into college as a freshman. We moved into the dorms.

The dorms were fun at first, but I didn't like the atmosphere. Everyone loved to drink, cuss, and mess around. I didn't, which is probably why I never made too many friends my freshman year.

My roommate loved to go party and have fun late and loved to come home around 1 or 2 in the morning while I was asleep. She would then do her homework with the lights on and talking to people.

I ended up hating how different we grew apart that year. We did get into a couple arguments towards the end, and then the very last quarter of school we didn't even make eye contact due to the difference in our personalities. She got on my nerves, and I got on her nerves. I tried to make her my friend, but she didn't like that idea, so we just continued to not be friends.

During the second quarter of school, Mitchel broke up with me over the phone. He told me that I should see other people, because I had only been with him my whole life. I was a wreck, and my roommate was no help because she hated me. I just cried myself to sleep that night, hoping he would call me but he never did.

About two days went by and then we got back together. He told me he was sorry, and I forgave him because I felt like I couldn't live without him.

I remember the same day he broke up with me; I failed my nutrition final for school. I got a D on the test. It sucked! I was so mad; I ended up failing that class with a C-. At UCLA, a C- is failing, so I was really pissed and took it pass or no pass, and accepted the no pass. I went through a lot of stress that day, and I hated college. I wanted to just give up, but I didn't. I just kind of kept to myself and didn't talk much.

No More Father

Later, during winter quarter, we were on a school break for a month. Christmas Day, Branden Sanders, my adopted father, passed away with cancer within a month of finding out he was diagnosed. We had no idea he was dying and he literally died faster than I could imagine. My grades dropped even more and I was so scared for my family and my grades in college. I thought I wouldn't make it to finish college.

His death dropped my heart to the ground. I loved him so much. He showed love in a different way. He didn't have to say the words, and he just showed he loved me and all of the children in the family. The entire family was devastated when we awoke that morning to realize that Branden was dead. From that day on, my mother was no longer the same, she was empty inside.

Christmas Eve was the night I will never forget. I went over to my boyfriend Mitchel's house to open presents as usual. I was sitting on a step watching everyone in his family open presents when all of the sudden I got this urge to run out of the house. I had no explanation except the gut feeling I held inside of my stomach. It was a striking shock in my body that made me run out of Mitchel's house. I got in my car and drove two streets over and ran inside my house. All I wanted to do was see my father. He could not stand or walk by this time. Within 24 hours he went from talking to bed ridden and sicker than ever. I dropped my bags at the front door and ran to my mom and dad's room. My dad was moaning and my mom and sister were cleaning his pants. He had an accident while I was gone. We called for a hospital bed, it was on its way.

"Dad!…Hi, Dad!" I jumped in and said to him as he was being held by my brother, mom, and sister to sit back down.

He looked up with little muscle in his eyes, and we stared at each other.

"I love you, Dad," I said softly as he bounced on the hospital bed that arrived at 11:00 p.m that night.

"I love you too…" he squeezed out with his last bit of energy.

That was the last talk my father and I had before I lost him forever. After the incident, we decided to go to bed as a family. My sisters Tiffany, Becca, Jessica, my mom and I slept in the same room as my dad. I had trouble sleeping that night because we woke up every couple hours to give him medicine to help him breathe. I also could not sleep because I had a bad feeling inside, and all I could do was listen to him breathe.

I remember Christmas Day at 5:30a.m. hearing his last raspy breath in the home hospital bed he was sleeping in. I knew it was his last breath because I stayed up all night listening for him to breathe. When I heard it stop, my heart stopped, and I began to cry.

"Mom, did you check on Dad?"

"Go to sleep quit worrying! Leave me and your father alone! Go back to bed!"

"Mom, really did you check Dad," as I started to cry.

"Oh, damn it, Amber." As she hopped out of bed with only half of her eyes open she walked over to his bed and grabbed his hand.

"Branden! Branden! Oh my God…I think…Branden No…No No No, Branden my baby Branden, baby, No!!! Ahhhhhh." She screamed as if she was dying.

"Mom, he's dead, Dad's dead." Tiffany my adopted sister cried as she held his wrist looking for a pulse.

All of my brothers and sisters jumped out of their bed and ran into my parents' bedroom; they all didn't know what happened. Jessica didn't even know he was dying.

"Jess, Dad died this morning," Becca said softly waking her up.

"Quit playing with me! Nice joke Becca! It's Christmas, move let me see for myself," as she pushed Becca out of the way.

"Dad? Oh My Gosh…No. Dad?" Jessica started to cry as she stood there staring at our father.

I didn't know what to do, so I put a blanket over his face. My mom yelled at me and said to leave him alone as she wiped the blood off of his face which had dripped out from passing away. I left the room and called all of my brothers and sisters that were older and told them to come over and see Dad before they took him away to be cremated. It was a long, very long day. I was broken. I didn't know how to react. My mother is the one who was hurt most, and she didn't want him to leave yet. We were not ready for such a fast death. We never celebrated Christmas that day. We celebrated it the next day and took his presents under the tree and set them aside. I tried to hide the ones that said Dad on them and didn't let my mom see them because they just made her choke up inside. We all opened presents happily to make my dad smile. We knew he was watching and we knew he didn't want us to be sad. He told us to have a big party for him if he ever died. So we did, we had a huge party for him at our house. That day of the party was the day I had ever seen so many people in one house. Everyone came to my dad's party to say goodbye and to be happy for his life. It was not the happiest party ever, but it was okay. I kept a smile on my face for him. His ashes were buried next to my mom's favorite hammock swing in the backyard with her garden flowers which she looks over every day.

No More Grandma

I was at the college campus, sitting in my dorm and my cell phone rang. I was tired, and I almost didn't pick it up, but I just rolled over and picked it up because I knew I was just being a lazy bum. Anyway, my mom calls and she sounded kind of raspy, and weird, like nothing I had ever heard before on the phone. I said, "Mom, what's up?"

She told me, "Amber, your grandmother died last night…"

There was silence on the phone. I just sat there in my dorm room looking down on the ground. *Did my mom just seriously say my grandma died?* I thought to myself as a tear slowly streamed out of the corner of my eye.

"Mom, what? You're kidding…No! Why? How?" I questioned.

"I don't know, Amber. Grandpa was ready to give her pills before he went to bed and when he went to give them to her he noticed she was not breathing."

"No way, oh my gosh, so what do we do now?"

"Well the service is on Wednesday, so can you come?"

"I have class, and I am not doing so well in it, and it is three hours long. I really shouldn't miss…I am almost failing that class. It is one of my hardest," I said in a concerned tone.

"It's okay, you don't have to come, it's not going to be that big of deal. Just go to class, we all understand. A lot of people can not come because they have other plans," my mom said in a positive voice.

I sat there and really thought if that sounded right. I was confused if I should go to her service or go to school and miss out on class. I told my mom, "Okay, well I will plan on going to class, and if I change my mind I will let you know."

We finished our conversation, and that was it. I sat on my bed all night thinking about my grandma. All I could think was sadness. I never really got to know my grandma Sanders because we never came to our grandparents' house very often. I do remember her always encouraging me though, in school and to go to church. I sat on my bed and remembered the time she got me my first flute in eighth grade. I needed one because I was moving on to high school, and I could no longer borrow the school's instrument. One day I went to visit them, and they had surprised me with a flute! I loved it, and played them a song that day. I remember feeling thought of by the Sanders grandparents and loved how they smiled when I would talk about anything.

After reminiscing about my grandparents and my grandma's sudden death, I just sat there on my bed with more tears falling down both cheeks. I was crying, but it had no pain like my sister's death or my father's death. This was a different kind of pain. I had pressure in my chest and burning in my eyes. I tried to hold it in, and thought it did not matter. *Another death,* I thought. *How do I react? My mother didn't sound all that concerned if I didn't even go to her service. Why wouldn't she be upset? Did it mean that much?* I was confused.

Wednesday came; I was sitting in women's studies looking at the clock. It had just struck 11:00. Class was starting, my teacher looked at me and said, "Amber, are you okay?"

My friends sitting next to me had known what had happened because I told them when I first sat in my seat. I asked their advice if I should stay in class because I am failing or if should I go to my grandmother's service. They looked at me like I was stupid. They said if I could make it I should go.

"Will you tell the professor that I am leaving due to a death? Thanks," I asked the girl to my right.

"Sure, go, hurry you still have time! You will make it," she said anxiously.

I told my professor that I was sorry, and I would make it up. She said it was alright.

Flying out of the bungalow down on ring road, I grabbed my blue bike and pedaled as fast as I could. *I am so stupid. I should have known. Why didn't I leave already? Oh, I hope I make it. I hope they understand. I can't believe I am about to miss my own grandmother's funeral service,* I thought to myself.

I called my brother Nathan, and told him I was on my way, and to wait up for me. He told me I would make it because the service started at 12:00 and I was only 40 minutes away. I felt nervous with rocks in my stomach. I pedaled my bike all the way to the other side of campus which took about 10 minutes and hooked my bike to a wall next to my car in the parking structure. I didn't really care where I put my bike, I had just wanted to get out of school as soon as possible so that I would make it.

I drove like a madman on the road. Swerving in and out of traffic with my mind all over the road, and focused mainly on the death of my grandma. I couldn't stop driving so fast. I wanted to be there so badly. I felt the adrenaline pumping in my forearms as a turned the wheels as I made it to the church.

I made it on time! Everyone was there, and it was only about 25 people all together. The service was weird and we all tried to follow the procedures. We had to take communion and read from the Bible. It was a different kind of church than I was used to. It was some kind with a letter P that I do not remember the name of. Very different might I say.

After the funeral service, we had a reception to the right of the church. We had finger sandwiches, pickles, fruit, and cake. After picking at the food, I talked to my grandpa. He seemed to have taken it all very well. He was calm and never cried or even made a tear. I tried to avoid the whole death topic, so we talked about school, like always. I told him how I was doing, and all I could think the whole time was that my grandpa had no one left at home to keep him company. I also thought that he just lost a son and a wife in less than six months! All I could think was about how lonely and sad my grandpa was going to be for a long time.

We talked a bit more about school because my grandfather loves to talk, and then I went to my aunt's house for another get together for the family. I went by myself because my mom and the other siblings had other things to do. We just talked about old memories since we hadn't seen much of each other in a long time.

Looking back on the two deaths in a very short time, I just tried to finish school because that was my priority. All I wanted to do was pass my classes. That's all I cared about at the moment. I was not in the mood to get A's and beat everyone in the class; I wanted to just get the hell out of school and rest in my bed all day long. I did that a lot, I ended up gaining about 10 pounds my freshman year because I would eat lunch, read a book on my bed and fall asleep. I was tired all the time, since I cried a lot by myself. I didn't do much work, except school work and lounge around in my dorm. That lasted for a good month. Then I got over it and moved to my mom's house for the summer.

The summer was not all that great for me. I went to work back at my old job from high school to make a little cash for my car and school stuff, but I was so bored. I would come to my mother's house just bored. There was nothing to do in the summer, but to lie around and eat. My mother and I got into arguments frequently and she started to make me pay rent for living there because we had no money for food in the house due to my father's death. I got mad and continued to argue back since I didn't like the fact that I had to pay rent. After all, I was the only one going to college, right? Well I guess I was not all that special because my mom needed me to help her out with just $150 a month. I soon realized I was just the same as everyone else in the house. It didn't really matter that I was in college, my dad died and my mom had no more income. I paid her, and then moved out that last August into an apartment next to campus.

Sophomore Year in College

Before my college life continued, I would like to mention that my brother Mathew (one year younger than me) was accepted into University of Southern California (USC) for the year of 2006. He found out that he had a talent to sing during high school and was taken aboard with a full music scholarship package to help him through college. He was lazy and forgot to fill out some papers to help him get where he is today, so that is where I came into play for him. I filled out his FAFSA and turned it in for him and I also applied for the CHAFEE grant (which is for former foster youth). He was thankful that I did that for him, but I know that if he didn't go onto college, he would have a hard life, so I knew I had to help. I did not want to see him end up in the streets ever again.

During my sophomore year I applied to be in Jumpstart, which is an after-school program for pre-school and got the opportunity to become a Corps Member! I was on my way to majoring in Social Science with a Public Community Service title, and a minor in education. I also got hired as an instructional aid for a pre-school in Irvine. I worked there the whole year and worked Jumpstart for a whole year. During my sophomore year in college I felt as if I needed to make up for the lack of accomplishment in my freshman year, so I did as much as I could to get ready for graduation and maybe travel and graduate school. I wasn't really interested in grad school, but I came to like the idea of eventually getting a master's in social work and working at Woodorange because that is where I came from. I also enrolled in a higher course for my major to get it out of the way, which became the hardest thing I had ever done in education. I wrote a small thesis. I conducted a research paper on after-school programs for minorities in education. It was a year-long research project and I wrote over 40 pages just in the final research paper. The end of my sophomore year was a blast. At the same time, very overwhelming and hard to do at once. I took 20 units most of the time, and bombarded my life with education and work. I think I liked it because it kept me focused. My last quarter of my sophomore year I had finally received straight A's. My head went through the roof when I found out. I was working so hard in school, which it all paid off. I was offered a TA position for the same research professor which I had that year, and I accepted it. I was also accepted into a graduate school preparation intensive five-week program from UCLA called Summer Enrichment Program (SEP). I joined the program that summer and almost died. I took 12 units in five weeks, wrote another research proposal on foster youth, and did a lot of work.

Yes, it was hard, but I found another piece of myself while in the program. I found more friends than I have ever met while in college. We all bonded as a family. Even the professors who taught us over eight hours a day came to love and adore all of us. It was the one time in my college life that the professors knew all of their 22 students by name. I remember one professor specifically too. He is not only a professor, but he was a very kind person. He reminded me of my father. He was stern, but showed love through other means, like buying us food every morning. He did not have to buy us goodies out of his own pocket, but he did. I grew to look up to him as an inspiration to be better in life. He is such a hard worker and devotes his time and self to his students, which is what I love about him. He makes me want to try my very best while in school and to not let anything get in my way.

When that summer program ended I had a nervous breakdown and was having panic attacks. I could not control how fast I was moving in life and college, that I was having trouble breathing. I was getting all of my anger, hate, and frustration built up, and then I released it by screaming.

Summer Entering My Junior Year

Mitchel came to pick me up the last day of the program and called me when he reached the parking lot. We were not all done saying our goodbyes so I sent him a text message saying that we were not done, so to wait a couple minutes. He waited, and then got a little too excited to see me and jumped out of his car. Meanwhile the car keys were in the ignition, with the air conditioner on full blast. He then slammed the car door to run and see me and said, "Oh crap!"

"What did you do?" I laughed.

"No, I think," as Mitchel reached for his car door, "No! I locked us out! Damn it!"

I was pissed. It was seriously about 100 degrees outside. I was all ready to go home and we had to sit on the curb waiting for AAA to come open the car.

Mitchel looked at me and said, "I don't even know how to act! Who are you? What happened?"

"Nothing, what are you talking about? I am me, nothing happened. What do you really think, not seeing me for five weeks changed the way you look and act towards me?"

"Well I guess not," Mitchel said as he grinned towards the ground.

We got the car unlocked about thirty minutes later and he drove me back to the apartment I was staying in, and we packed up to go home finally. I rented a dolly to load all of my belongings, and Mitchel stuffed it all on one cart for one trip! It was stacked so high, when he turned the corner of the apartment everything leaned toward the left of us and suddenly fell over.

I screamed, "Uh why is this happening? Are you really that stupid? Come on!"

I instantly blew up. I started feeling my heart pound. I got light headed and dizzy. "What is happening to me, I feel sick," I said to Mitchel.

Mitchel turned to give me a hug to calm me down. "Get off of me! Uhhh don't touch me! I don't want a hug can't you see?" I screamed.

Mitchel's face went blank. He didn't know what to do. "Babe, what's wrong with you? You need to calm down."

I went to sit on my bed. My roommate told me I was having a panic attack, but I didn't believe her. I just sat there with a pillow in my face. I screamed into it not knowing why I felt so ruined. My roommate then told me to calm down and to breathe. She told me to count, and to get my mind off of everything. I took a deep breath, but nothing changed. I just sat on the end of my bed and eventually got up and finished moving. That was the last day of the program. I had relief as I looked out of my car window looking back at the "boot camp" thinking it was all over, no more work.

I took one week off after that program, went to my mom's house to chill out and then enrolled in summer session two and worked as an instructional assistant for special ed pre-school for the summer. My mom yelled at me for enrolling in school for the summer session II, since I stressed myself out and freaked out during the intense summer program I had just finished. I told her that I can not live alone, so I must keep myself busy. If I sit at home alone and just work a couple of days of the week, I will die. I hate to be alone. Maybe it is a weird thing that I have acquired since I was little, but I absolutely hate it. So I took on another class and worked full time.

Summer 2007

It is August 13, 2007, I have rested from boot camp now, and I am enrolled in more summer classes at UCLA, and I will continue to work with pre-school children. Today, I just got back from a camping trip in Arizona with Mitchel and his family. We went to Colorado River and had lots of fun. We got home around 5:30pm. Mitchel needed gas so we went to COSTCO to fill up, and then he was going to take me to my mom's house in La Hibra to get my car that I left. When we turned on the street to get my car, my mom was in her car leaving to the mall. She saw Mitchel's car and made a U-turn. She met up with us at the house and said she was lonely so she was going to the mall to get a cookie (even though she is diabetic). She told me she felt like being bad, because no one was home. My little sister, Jessica, went to summer camp for a week, and my brother Nathan who is living in my mom's house was at work. Becca was staying the day with her best friend. My mom was just going out to get out of the empty house. I decided that I would stay and visit because she was lonely. We were all hungry so we went to KFC and ate at the restaurant there because it was really hot outside and we don't have air conditioning. When we were ordering our food my mother hugged me from behind and smiled. "I love you, baby," she said in a sweet voice.

She gave me tingles all over my arms because I knew what she meant, and it felt so passionate from her heart. I felt the love, it was really an indescribable moment.

After eating, my plans were to go back to UCLA and get ready for school the next day. When I pulled up to the house to drop my mom and Mitchel off and go back to Irvine, I said, "Well I am full, and I feel like a fatty so I am going to visit just a little longer to make my stomach feel a little better."

My mom was delighted I could see it in her face. Although, she did say, "Amber, don't feel that you have to stay to keep me company, Nathan will be home soon, so go home before it is dark and get settled in for school."

"No, Mom. I know, but I want to stay a little longer, promise."

"Okay then, come in, sweetie," replied my mom.

I ended up staying at my mom's house until around 8:00pm, and then I decided I should go back to Los Angeles to get all of my homework ready and clothes set out for class in the morning. It was dark, and not much traffic was out. It was still about 78 degrees outside so I had my air on in my car blowing in my face with my NOW 25 CD playing in the background. I was flying down Imperial Boulevard when all of the sudden I see my brother Allan walking along the side of a motel looking through some bushes. My instant reaction was to stop and pull over to get him. In the back of my mind I was thinking, *Oh my gosh! That's my brother! I need to get him help.* I had lost Allan for a good couple of months since he was kicked out of the house on his 18th birthday for doing drugs. He was homeless, and was just walking the streets. I hit the brakes and drove into an opening and was within distance to see Allan. I honked once, he stopped. I honked twice and he started to walk closer to me looking confused. I rolled down my car window and waved my hand to come closer. He didn't know who was in the car so I yelled, "Allan! Get it, it's me."

He walked a little faster towards me. He was squinting as if he had sun in his eyes. He was just trying to see who I really was in the car that just pulled up out of nowhere. As he was walking towards me, I saw his skinny legs and thin face and just thought to myself that I must help this boy. After coming closer, Allan reaches for the door and gets in. He just sat there and smiled. I started to cry and told him that I had something to give him, but it was in my apartment in Irvine. I said, "Where are you going, Allan?"

"Nowhere, I was waiting for a bus, but the bus stop I was at the bus never came. I wasn't going anywhere. My friend gave me a free day pass so I was riding the bus around."

"Well, do you want to come over to Irvine to get this card I have for you? It is from the CEO of Woodorange Children's foundation. You know, where we came from? The man told me there is a program to help former foster youth to get housing and a job, stuff like that. Are you interested and willing to change and get off drugs?"

Allan smirked and said, "Sure...I guess."

"When is the last time you did a drug?" I asked.

"Today," Allan said.

"Where? How do you get it?"

"Amber it's everywhere! I can get my marijuana anywhere anytime…for free!" he explained.

"Did you eat today?" I asked in a concerned voice.

"Well, yeah I had candy and chips," Allan said.

"Where did you get that? Did you steal it from a store?" I asked.

"Yeah, dude the 99 Cent store and the Dollar Tree are so easy to steal from, I eat there all the time with my friends. We jack all kinds of stuff. They don't have cameras. It's so easy!" Allan exclaimed.

"Well, I am taking you home, feeding you some food, get you a shower, and then I will have to take you to UCLA tomorrow because I have class, and then we are going to Woodorange to get you help, okay?"

"Alright," Allan sighed looking out the car window to his right watching the traffic flow by.

We arrived at my apartment in Los Angeles, California, and my roommate was home. I told Allan to wait outside and I talked to her explaining the whole situation. She was fine with letting him in, and we went through the door and sat down.

I then cooked him a frozen burrito and gave him Oreos and water. I gave him a towel to take a shower with and a clean shirt to wear to bed. He slept on the couch that night. We filled out paperwork to get help until midnight, and then we went to bed. I locked my room door because I didn't know if he would steal from me or not. I had a good feeling he was telling me the truth, but I had no idea how he was from being off the streets and on drugs. I almost thought he would walk out in the middle of the night and not want the help I offered to him. I was tossing and turning in my bed picturing us going to Woodorange and explaining our situation to get help. I couldn't sleep much and eventually I went to bed around 3:00 that night, or morning shall I say.

The next day, August 14, 2007, I took Allan to class (UCLA) and let him sit in the back filling out a paper I needed from him. I told him to write me his life story on a piece of paper for me. He drew a devil on the front and wrote me a couple paragraphs. I told him to write a lot, and he wrote only one page.

After class, we drove to Taco Bell as I was talking to people from Woodorange in the car to set an appointment for Allan. No one picked up, so I told Allan that we will just show up at Woodorange's door step and ask for help personally. He agreed and we drove to Santa Ana, California, after we ate a grilled stuffed burrito and nachos.

We arrived to Woodorange and there were lots of people to help. They showed us all around and showed all of the resources Allan and I could use to get help. They told Allan he could get free food, clothes, and find a job there. We were excited. We spent four long hours that day sitting in a resource center filling out paperwork for different agencies to get help. We applied for everything he was eligible for. After all was done, Woodorange helped us get in nice dress clothes to go get a job.

I drove Allan to Anaheim, California, for a job interview that day. This place hires people with past problems such as drugs and convictions. I thought it was a good place to take him, so I did. The lady interviewed him until around 6:30pm. We told her everything, and she felt like she would help us so she told us to get the right papers and documents to get him started.

After the interview, I drove him to his grandparents' house, where they said he could stay for two days. I was concerned about the two-day limit so I went inside and met the family he came from, and I introduced myself and told them what we did all day. I talked to them until 9:00pm. We had a very long discussion about Allan and how to help him. I explained all of the resources available and they were all shocked. They never knew the amount of help one person could get if they just looked into it. They fed Allan and me turkey burgers and lemonade. I then left and said my goodbyes and told Allan I would call him every night at 7:00 pm to see how his day went. He agreed, and I drove home and went to bed to get ready for work the next day. I was tired, and passed out on my bed.

Still Summer

It is now August 20, 2007, well, the weekend is over. It was short for me; I had a very tiring week last week trying to help Allan to get off the streets and to get help. I was calling him every day, but I actually didn't call him on Saturday. I should have though; he didn't go to a meeting he was supposed to. I was mad, but then I told him that he needs to remember because I can only remember so much, and I have enough going on that I can't do it all. I think he is getting it now. He is realizing that he needs to do some of his work as well.

My diabetic, osteoporosis mother fell during the week and almost broke her arm, but I guess her medication is kicking in better since she is exercising regularly and doing better with herself. Although...I did have to take a whole bag of Albertson's fresh baked chocolate cookies from her on Saturday night. She was eating sugar! I told her, "Mother! No more chocolate, I am taking them away! I am going to hide them!"

"No!...Fine, yeah you should because they are bad for me," my mom said sarcastically.

After the cookie incident, I decided to help my little sister Jessica lose some weight. She is bigger than me, and I am eight years older than her. I decided to make a plan for her. I told her that if she lost six pounds by the next time I see her, I will give her a brand new hair straighter over $75.00 with a five-year warranty. She agreed with joy, but did not follow through for the first two days. She ate Oreos, Mac N' Cheese, tons and tons of butter on her corn for dinner, and other crazy foods which I told her not to have.

On Sunday afternoon, I thought Mitchel was going to break up with me because I had a severe case of PMS. I was mad at everyone and cranky. Why? No reason, I was just going through my time of the month. I get so mean sometimes, and I don't mean most of what I say, I just say it. I told Mitchel he had a pea brain because we were driving around town, and he kept getting lost because we were talking. I couldn't believe that talking distracted him so much, so I yelled at him. We got over it eventually after bickering for a good 10 minutes. He almost kicked me out of his car, but I didn't let him until he calmed down. Later on Sunday, we apologized and said our goodnights. We decided we no longer like fighting, so we are going to work on it, because we are getting nowhere.

One Monday I went to work. I work at a pre-school in Los Angeles, California, with special education children. I love them, but they are a lot of work. I have to chase them, carry them, feed them, change them, and more. I think I want to teach special education if the time comes around for me one day because I really love children.

After work, I went to Target and picked up some bathroom stuff like shampoo and face moisturizer. I was so hungry when I got in my car, but I told myself to eat at home because I had spent too much in Target. I can never leave without buying everything I see. The stupid little clearance and "price cut" signs get me every time. I always think I am getting a good deal, when later I wonder if I really needed that DVD or that candy I purchased.

After coming home I made some rice and chicken and ate it on my couch while watching a TV show on young girls influencing others around the world. I thought to myself that I was going to be one of those girls one day. I really want to help foster children one day and give them all the help I can when I have the resources available to me. During the TV show I got many phone calls on my cell phone about Allan from Woodorange, and I used another 50 minutes talking to people. I swear, during this month I have used more minutes on my cell phone than I have ever used in my life, just talking to representatives from different agencies to help Allan. I have spent a lot of money and time, oh and gas to help my brother, but I do believe that it has all been worth it. I think he will pull through with the help I am giving him. Well I can only hope.

The month is September of 2007. I start school soon, and I can't wait. Only two more years at UCLA. Today was so boring for me. I was sitting in my apartment doing absolutely nothing because summer school is over and fall quarter has not started yet. I applied to some summer programs for 2008 and watched a lot of television.

I have now come to realize that myspace.com is new way of living for everyone in this world. It is pretty crazy how people get so wrapped up in that lame website. I even catch myself stuck on that thing for a long time. Why I ask? Because it is a time sucker! It loves to take over your life! Scary I know, but it is true. I was trying to think the other day what life would be like without myspace.com, and I thought it would be very different. It would also probably reduce the drama in everyone's life by at least 75%. My roommates, friends, family, my friend's family, parents, co-workers, teacher, and many more people I have met throughout my life have a myspace! It is ridiculous. I have actually even heard of people going on other people's myspace to look at their profile before they get hired for a job. Now that is crazy. I even saw presidential candidates on there! Now what has our world become?

Who I Am Now

I am now working on many tasks in my life, because I am preparing to go on to graduate school to study the foster care system. All of these past experiences that I have explained are deeply imbedded in my heart, but I have realized with time and maturity that life happens, and you have to accept it and move on by taking one day at a time. I finally know who I want to be and where I want to go in life. I had the opportunity to see the depressing side of life with alcohol and drugs, which has inspired me to rise above and take it as a learning experience. I developed an interest in foster youth, education and social work while going through Woodorange and different foster homes. While attending the University of California, Los Angeles, I have learned my responsibilities for who I represent. I want to give back to my community and implement what I have learned to the future foster youth society. I want to give back the knowledge in which I have had the opportunity of receiving. I hope to be a mentor for other foster youth who may have lost hope or who do not see the future ahead. Attending UCLA has been my dream that has finally come true, which is why I want to share my experiences with others to encourage them to strive for the best.

In addition to obtaining my B.S. in social science by 2009, I will have specialized in Public and Community Service (PCS) and have minored in education. With the specialization in PCS, it has offered me an opportunity to learn about public and community issues by working in designated community agencies and government organizations that apply academic theories and analytical skills to the solution for real-world problems. The program helped me develop a better understanding of integrating academia and service into my community. The specialization helped me identify and analyze socially significant needs addressed in the community in the context of many social science disciplines. Within the PCS specialization, I completed a research project and paper as well as 200 hours of participant observation and analysis, 300 hours of community service, and 200 hours of an internship at Woodorange Children's Foundation. I researched Latina/o education in after-school programs in the city of Santa Ana, California. I was also privileged to work with Dr. Janette Cast during my specialization of PCS. I also became Dr. Cast's teacher's assistant during my junior year. I gained a closer academic relationship with her as well as a better understanding of pursuing higher education. I also committed to a year study on foster youth and high education for my honors thesis during my junior year. Lastly, I have taken a full year of statistics, research methods, and attended a Summer Bridge Program as well as the Summer Academic Enrichment Program (SAEP) at UCLA to prepare me for higher education. In the SAEP program, I studied foster youth and wrote a research proposal while preparing for graduate school including: intermediate statistics, communications, and research methods classes. SAEP was a rigorous twelve-unit, five-week program, which advanced my research skills as well as public speaking skills to better prepare me for higher education. I also decided to write my honors thesis on higher education for foster youth during my junior year, and learned a lot as I researched many other former foster youth's experiences. While doing all of these tasks simultaneously, I was also a part of the Associated Student body for UCLA, a board member for Community Service Leadership Program, and served on a committee for former foster youth to help make changes in California.

My short-term goals are to attend a graduate program that will allow me to conduct extensive research on foster care and social work and later on education. I am very passionate about extending my knowledge about foster care systems and youth. While I am in the program, I am going to work at a children's foundation that has to deal with foster care. My long-term goals are to graduate with a master's or doctorate in social work and work in administration for a foster care or home foundation. I also plan to further my education after I receive more experience in the field of foster care. It would be an honor to make an impact on society by establishing new policies and making a greater chance for success in future foster children. I was recently (2008) admitted into Harvard University to study and research public policy and to look deeper into the issue of foster care. When the time comes, I want to be a professor and help shape society as well. I plan to give back to my community because I want to help those who I can truly relate to.

Ending Remarks

Going through my junior year in college has been tough for me. I may get wrapped up in academics and organizations, but it does not cover my past. Some days I think about it, and most days I don't, but when I do, it hurts. I hate the fact that I will no longer have some of my family in my life due to death. It crushes me to think about it all. I try to stay active in school so that I can put my stress elsewhere. I may try hard, but emotionally I still have to cope with a lot of things that come up on different days of the year, such as Christmas, or birthdays. Some days I wake up sad or just have sad moments when I can not stop thinking about my past and present. This is something that I am still working on, and I am hoping it will pass as I get older.

Also, having so much on my plate has given me a head full of stress and pressure. When I try to go to bed at night, sometimes I can not sleep because I think of too many things in my mind. I am so busy that I think of the day, how it went, the next day, and how I am going to plan for it. Now I sound like a crazy person! I have also experienced massive headaches from stress so bad that I cannot sleep. I have had to get out of bed and take a hot bath to soothe the pain, but it comes right back. Some days I work off of no sleep, and it is painful. I cannot help it though, I love everything that I am involved in, and I want to help make a difference so that others can understand that life will be okay.

I have also wondered how my mom adopted five children. Two of them did not want to take the path of a fulfilling life, and they take the easy way out. I also wonder how the other half made it through all of the trauma and misery in life and have dreams. We all came from the same family around the same age, yet we all have different passions and dreams for life. Some have accepted that they do not want to go to college, and some have committed to not ever repeating the past. This amazes me, how lives can be ruined by past mistakes, or how lives can be turned around from the past mistakes of life.

Mitchel (my boyfriend of now 4 years) pointed out to me something I had never thought of. He told me that all I do is boss people around, always like to be in charge, and I am a mother figure to a lot of people. Some people, no...most people hate that aspect about me, and so do I because sometimes I feel like I have to help others. Mitchel told me that the reason why I am the way I am is because I have never been a child. I was forced to always be the mother and to make sure everyone was safe and doing what they were supposed to do. I agree. I have this urge to jump in on people's work and nag at them when they are not on task. I can't help it sometimes, but I am working on it. I sometimes wish I could have my childhood back, but there is nothing I can do about it, and now I am on my own and fully support myself. I pay for everything, cook on my own, and drive to work on my own. It seems like the childhood years passed me up, and now all I can do is move forward. It's okay with me though. I love how things happened for a reason in my life, and I truly believe that. There is nothing I can do about my past, but learn from it, and move forward.

This is a short story because I am not that old. I will continue to write as my life ages. I also wish to add any memories as they come to me. Many children going through foster care take different routes in life. My direction in life was given to me at birth. I knew since I was little that I would not let anything get in my way. Some people are born with different traits. Not all get a chance like I did or the opportunity. I know that Nathan, Mathew, Jessica, and I will make it throughout our tough life because we will not repeat an ugly life cycle as we were given. I can see the drive and motivation that we all have in ourselves. Yes, we were all born with drugs and alcohol in the womb of our birth mother, but we were saved by the miracles of life, which is why we are all so strong. I have made a commitment to steer clear from alcohol, smoking, and drugs because I know I have a family history of the substances. The doctors have said that all of us may be highly susceptible to alcohol or drugs due to our pregnancy stories, but I will not let that affect me. All children who have gone through the foster care system have experienced many different stories, memories, and tragedies. It's what you do with your experiences to make you who you are today. I will leave you with this: we can only push forward, not pull from our past. I thank everyone who helped me along the way. I know I have a lot of plans ahead of me, but it is because of the people in my life who gave me love and support.

About the Author

Kimberly Snodgrass is a current honors social science undergraduate student at the University of California, Irvine, where she researches former foster youth and their educational paths. Snodgrass' goal is to promote successful foster youth and to inform the world about the academic hardships placed on foster youth today. Snodgrass plans to complete further research on foster care and higher education as she moves forward towards graduate school.